Lesso

A·Novella of Alte

Julie Mannino

Author's Note

This novel contains content intended for mature readers. It includes bi-awakening, coercion, Professor/student, caning, light bondage, and an age gap. It's set in 1695 in Camaday.

For info on the latest books, including queer fairy tales, fantasy, and M/M romance, sign up here for the Newsletter.

Table of Contents

This is the life and the way that was chosen.

"Learn everything you can, anytime you can, from anyone you can. There will always come a time when you will be grateful you did."
-Sarah Caldwell

Arthur's Lesson

Arthur slung his arm around Jane's shoulders. "Come on, let's go outside. We can go around back."

"I'm not sucking you off back there. It's gross."

"You've done it before."

She made a face. "I feel like a corner whore when we do stuff outside."

"Well...we don't have a lot of options," said Arthur. "Unless you want to find a spot on the beach."

"Too much walking, and I'd rather go to your room," she said. "Then we can use the bed."

"You know we can't do that," said Arthur.

"It's only a problem if we're found out." She raised an eyebrow.

Arthur suppressed a sigh as he picked up his wineglass. The tavern was full of other students, but he tuned out the chatter as he fidgeted with the stem of his glass. He just wanted to get sucked off. Actually, he wanted more, but Jane wouldn't go all of the way with him. Behind the tavern wasn't the best place, but trying to sneak her into his room at Boston College was asking for trouble.

"Your roommate is cute," said Jane's latest friend as she leaned an elbow on the scuffed table. Arthur had already forgotten her name. "You know, maybe Jasper would like a break from studying tonight." She bit her lip and giggled.

"He probably would," said Arthur.

If she was willing to suck off Jasper, or at least give him a handjob, he'd owe Arthur big time. And maybe, just maybe, Jane would let Arthur go a little further if they were in a comfy spot. He'd get in huge trouble if he was caught, but he also wanted to fuck. He fiddled with the gold earring in his ear as Jane gave him an expectant look.

Maybe the guard in front of their dorm would be willing to take a little walk.

"Fine," Arthur said as he leaned back and straightened his cloak. "I'll bribe the guard at ten to go away for a bit."

"We'll be there," said Jane, and her friend nodded.

The College had only started allowing women back about four years ago in 1691, and they had a strict rule against either side mingling in their rooms. Who knew what improper things would happen?

But the guard outside of the men's dorm would surely take a bribe and fuck off for a bit. Arthur and his friend, Jasper, had noticed before that he sometimes walked around a bit at the front to stretch his legs. He could go a little further and keep his head turned away too.

**

Around nine that night, Arthur went downstairs and found the night guard in his usual spot.

"Erm, I wanted to ask you something."

The guard leaned back in his chair as the lantern on the ground by his boots flickered. "Is someone causing trouble in there?"

"No, no. I wanted to ask if you could take a real slow walk around the dorm at ten. And maybe you could take another midnight."

Two hours would be plenty of time to fool around. Arthur fingered the coins in his pocket as the guard peered at him.

"How about no? I think my legs are feeling tired tonight."

"Aw, come on," said Arthur. There was no rule against someone being out at ten, but if the ladies saw the guard upfront, they'd never be stupid enough to try and walk by him to come in.

"No women in the men's room, and no men in the women's rooms," said the guard. "I know what you're up to, and I think that rule is pretty clear."

"What's your name?" asked Arthur.

"Will."

Arthur pushed up his spectacles. "I'll pay you, Will. I'm sure guards aren't paid enough for this sort of work."

"It's not exactly dangerous here."

"Still, maybe you've got a sweetheart. You could buy her a present."

"I don't have one."

Arthur pulled out two shillings, hoping the sight of the money would lure him. "You could buy yourself something."

"Nah, I'm good."

Arthur almost groaned at the idea of seeing Jane tomorrow after this failure. He'd said he'd do it and acted all sure of himself. "You'd just have to take a walk at ten and again at midnight."

The guard rubbed his scruffy chin as he looked at the coins. "How badly do you want this?"

"Really bad." Arthur figured he'd have to go upstairs and get more money. Hell, if that was the case, Jasper better pay a bit too.

"Come around the side." The guard stood.

"Er, why?"

"Because I said so."

Arthur followed him around the side of the building. It was dark, and clusters of neatly trimmed bushes made a line along the side. The guard led Arthur behind them. If he wanted some ridiculous amount of money, why couldn't he just say so? It's not like anybody was listening up front.

"You want this real bad, right?" asked Will.

"Yeah," said Arthur. "If two shillings isn't enough, I can possibly get you a couple more if I ask-"

"I'll take the two shillings, but you have to suck me off too."

Arthur's face grew hot. "Excuse me?"

"You'll get on your knees and suck my cock," said Will. "Or are you still a virgin that doesn't even know what that means?"

"Yes, I know what it means!" hissed Arthur. "But I'm not gay, and I don't even know how."

"You better be ready to learn if you want me to take a little walk later. You don't have to be gay anyway. Just do a passable job and swallow my load."

Arthur couldn't properly make out Will's expression in the dark, but with the moonlight, he saw him fold his arms. "That's disgusting to ask of me."

"Then no deal," said Will.

"Just take the money. It's two whole shillings. I'll ask Jasper for a couple as well. That's a good bit of money for something so easy that hardly requires any real effort."

"I could get fired if I was found out," said Will.

"Say you had to piss or that-that you had to go to the privy and sit."

"Or you could save your roommate two shillings and swallow me."

"I'll tell the Head Dean that you propositioned me!"

"I'll tell him that you offered to suck me off and pay me so you could sneak a girl up. You know how strict he is. You already got in trouble for making out with some lady in the library and getting a handjob. This will likely get you kicked out."

"It was behind the library," snapped Arthur.

"The problem is, I think the Head Dean will believe me, not you," said Will. "Besides, a blowjob isn't that hard unless you're too much of a fancy college boy to get on your knees for me. It's that, or no snatch for you tonight."

Arthur clutched the coins and was about to walk away, but he thought about tomorrow. Jane would see him in class or the library, and she'd probably shake her head and roll her eyes because he hadn't been able to do what he said he'd do. Maybe she'd start talking to that other guy in Latin who had a big house of his own in the city. Nobody was guarding his front door and forbidding ladies from entry.

Damn it. He just wanted to have as much fun as possible here before he was done with College. He'd kick himself in the ass if he didn't finally get up Jane's skirts.

Maybe it wouldn't be that bad. Will probably wouldn't last that long and must be desperate if he was propositioning some twenty-one-year-old student. It didn't mean Arthur was gay if it was just a one-time thing, right? When it came to sex, all he thought about was how far his current interest would let him go. And his current interests were never men.

He could do this for the possibility of sex with Jane.

"Okay, fine," he snapped.

"Give me the money." Will held out his hands for the coins.

This was like backward prostitution. Arthur gave him the two shillings and stood there as the awkwardness of the whole thing was suddenly unbearable.

Will started fiddling with his trousers. "Get on your knees. Your mouth can't reach my dick from there."

Arthur's face flushed as he got on his knees. Something bobbed in front of his face, and he still hesitated until Will spoke again.

"I guess I should go tell the Head Dean."

Arthur fumbled for the base of the guard's dick. "No! I'll do it."

As soon as he got his lips around the head, Will batted off his hand. "No hands."

Arthur couldn't believe he had a man's dick in his mouth. The swollen head had made the foreskin retract, and as he half-heartedly licked at it, he felt the slit and tasted pre-cum. Jane wasn't lying when she said it was rather salty.

Will grabbed his hair and pushed his head down further. "Is that how you like a woman to suck you off? You better do a good job, or I'll still tell the Head Dean. I better not feel your teeth either."

Arthur couldn't reply with his mouth full. The tip touched the back of his throat, and he almost gagged. Shit. That was why Jane didn't like it when he'd tried to push her head down once.

Will tightened his grip. "Think about what you like, and do that. No hands."

Arthur licked at the underside. Oh my God, he was really doing this.

"Hollow those cheeks," growled Will.

Arthur bobbed his head as he sucked and used his tongue on the underside. He always liked it when Jane did it at a steady rhythm. Will's cock was veiny, and he could feel the little ridges.

"You're not so bad for a fancy college boy," grunted Will. "I bet you've done this before. You probably trade blowjobs for essays or whatever."

Arthur's reply came out garbled, and Will fisted his hair again. He almost choked as the head pushed into his throat.

"Don't talk. Use that tongue."

Arthur, with his nose buried in the guard's pubes, lapped at the underside near the base. Will pulled him back a little for air and pushed him right back down.

"That's it," he murmured. "Just relax."

Arthur tongued the thick shaft as Will's head blocked his airway. Relaxing was a struggle when he was a little afraid he'd throw up. Will repeated the action a couple of more times and held his head down again.

"Keep using that tongue. Don't stop or the deal's off."

It wasn't quite as bad now, although Arthur preferred having air. Will breathed heavier as Arthur dared to look up.

"Good job. See? You learn fast."

Arthur's cock twitched in his trousers, and shame rose in his stomach a moment later. He wasn't supposed to like this or find it arousing. Not even a little.

Will pulled him off and slapped his cock on the side of Arthur's face. "You like this, don't you?"

"No," he said even though his dick threatened to swell.

"I guess I should tell the Head Dean."

"I mean, y-yes. I like it."

"You like what?" Will smeared his spitty shaft on Arthur's face.

He'd never had anything so degrading done to him, and his dick kept thickening. "I like sucking your cock."

"You should love it."

"I love sucking it."

Will rubbed the exposed head across Arthur's lips, and he darted his tongue out, eager to taste it again.

What the hell was wrong with him?

"Tell me how badly you want my cock," whispered Will.

"I want it."

"I think you can do better than that."

"I want your cock in my mouth. Please let me suck it." The moist head rubbed on the other side of his face, and he felt the chilly night air on the spit and pre-cum left on his cheek. "I want your cum in my mouth. Please, Will."

Arthur's dick was fully erect in his trousers. All he could think about was having Will's back in his mouth so he could tongue the veins and hear him growl again. He was tempted to fist himself too. What would it be like to cum as he sucked and tasted the guard's load in his mouth?

"Open," ordered the guard, and Arthur eagerly complied.

Will started a punishing pace that made Arthur's eyes water as his cock strained at his trousers, and he couldn't help the noise of appreciation that he made. He flicked his tongue while the guard thrusted in his mouth. Arthur found himself with his nose buried in the guard's pubes again as he lapped at the base.

He might have been on his knees with his mouth being used like a two-bit whore, but he was the one making Will breathe and swear like he was close.

"Stick your tongue out," Will ordered as he withdrew.

Arthur didn't think twice. He obeyed, and he felt the head on his tongue a moment later as Will jerked himself. Seconds later, Arthur tasted cum.

"Fuuuck, yes," snarled Will.

The salty fluid kept coming as Arthur collected each spurt with his head tilted up. Will shuddered as the last drops came out before he grabbed Arthur's chin with one hand.

"Keep it in your mouth and taste it," said Will. "You like that, don't you?"

To Arthur's shame, he did. He rolled the thick fluid in his mouth and felt wetness on his own cock head as pre-cum dribbled out.

"Swallow it," said Will.

Arthur felt the cum slide down his own throat. For the first time ever, he'd swallowed a man's load.

And he'd loved it.

"If you ever want to bring a lady up, this is what you'll do for me," Will said as he let go. "And if you don't want me to tell the Head Dean anyway tomorrow morning, you'll come down after midnight when your girl leaves so you can suck me off again. I'll take a walk at ten, and again at midnight. You better be down before twelve-thirty."

"My roommate-" started Arthur, wondering what excuse he could possibly use for leaving their room so late.

Will grabbed his chin. "You'll be down before twelve-thirty, and this is what will happen every time you want to bring a woman to your room. You better think in the future about whether you're willing to give me two blowjobs in a night or have the Head Dean find out." He slipped a finger in Arthur's mouth, and he automatically sucked. "I don't think that'll be a problem, will it?"

"No," Arthur said around his finger as his untouched cock ached with want.

"Good."

Will removed his finger, fixed his trousers, and walked away. He didn't even ask if Arthur wanted his cock sucked. He'd have Jane for that, but still.

As he remained on his knees, almost too shocked to move, he realized maybe he didn't care if she came up. In fact, he couldn't wait to come down later and give Will another blowjob behind the bushes. What the hell? He'd never thought about men before.

He stood and adjusted himself, willing his raging erection to calm down. Maybe he liked both, but other guys always talked about women and chased after them, so he'd simply been doing the same for years. He'd never questioned being straight.

A man that was truly straight would never find sucking a dick so enjoyable, right?

It had been repulsive at first, but it had been new and unfamiliar. He'd do it again if he could to have the feel of a shaft filling his mouth and taste the cum.

In fact, if Jane lost interest in him, Arthur would still let the guard fuck his mouth even without the added bonus. He'd do it for the simple pleasure of having another man using his mouth. Maybe Will would rub his cock on Arthur's face again.

He couldn't wait to come down after midnight.

Jasper's Lesson

Jasper wasn't even sure if he wanted to fool around with the woman who was busy unbuttoning the top of her dress.

"The best way to learn anatomy is to have a hands-on lesson," she purred.

Jasper wasn't taking anatomy this year, but she clearly didn't care. She was already climbing on top of him, and he reached up to grasp her breasts. Hearing Arthur and Jane on the other side of the curtain that divided the room was a bit of a mood killer.

"I'll pull out before I cum," pleaded Arthur.

"Pfft. I'm not taking that risk."

"Come on. Do you know what I had to do to let you come up here?"

Jane made a noise of derision. "What? Did you pay the guard a couple shillings? That's hardly worth the risk of me getting pregnant. The physician's bill after my Father got through with you would be a lot higher."

"I'm on the herbs," Jasper's lady whispered.

She felt good against him, but he'd almost rather go upstairs and have a session with the guy on the top floor even though they hadn't talked in a while. He liked women, but he preferred dicks. The problem with his old fuck buddy was that he always seemed ashamed afterward like Jasper was some dirty secret that he didn't want to look at or think about once he got his rocks off.

Of course, they probably would both be kicked out of Boston College if they were found out to be gay. None of the men in their building would want them around. The horror. A gay man might have looked at their ass once.

Besides, this lady seemed willing to go all the way, and it'd be nice to think about something besides the stack of books on his desk and how he needed to make his poems for English flow better.

"I'm going to make you scream my name," the lady whispered as she rubbed his erection through his trousers.

Would this be a bad time to mention that he'd already forgotten her name?

The door suddenly opened, and he nearly shoved the woman off of him when he recognized the man's pale blonde hair. Arthur made a noise and clothes rustled from beyond the curtain.

"What the hell do you think you're doing?" asked Ezra.

Jasper's woman gasped as she scrambled off of the bed and hurried to redo the buttons on her dress.

"This is not what it looks like!" babbled Arthur. "I swear, she's just helping me find something that...I dropped."

Jasper wanted to smack his forehead.

Ezra leaned on the door frame. "Besides the fact that there's to be no mingling of males and females in your room, I know exactly what you all were doing. Who's responsible for this? One of you must have had the bright idea of waiting until the guard went to take a piss or something."

Jasper's heart pounded as he sat up. It had been entirely Arthur's idea, and he'd paid off the guard to take a little "walk" at ten so the ladies could sneak in.

"It was my idea," Jasper blurted out.

The Professor's greyish-blue eyes went right to his face, and he felt himself flush. Why did they have to get caught by the Professor whom he often fantasized about when he had no option but his hand? Hell, he'd even thought about Ezra a few times when he'd been getting pounded by his fuck buddy.

His pale hair, toned figure, and eyes often invaded Jasper's thoughts even though he knew he shouldn't be thinking about a Professor in such a manner.

"This was your idea?" asked Ezra.

"Yeah, and he didn't even know about it, and I asked the ladies to come up. I mean..." Jasper let out a nervous chuckle. "What was he supposed to do when Jane got into his bed? Say no?"

Arthur started to say something, but Ezra held up a hand to him as he pursed his lips and focused on Jasper. "You know the rules."

"I'm sorry, Professor Oakley," said Jasper. The English Professor was usually laid back and let the students call him by his first name, but this definitely wasn't the time.

"I don't think sorry cuts it." Ezra glanced at the women. "You two need to get out. Now. The next time a man asks you to his room, you'd better say no. You certainly won't be allowed to stay and continue your studies if you get pregnant, and we don't need furious parents storming up here if they find their daughter's virtue has been messed with."

The women had fixed their clothes, and they hurried past the Professor with bowed heads and hushed apologies.

"Jasper, come with me," said Ezra. "Arthur, maybe you should have a talk later with your roommate about following the rules." He stepped into the hallway."

"Wait, Jasper-" started Arthur.

"You should probably finish your Latin homework," Jasper said before he hurried out and shut the door so Arthur wouldn't blurt out the truth.

Without a word, Ezra turned, and Jasper followed. He was probably going to get his ear chewed off with a long lecture about rules and morals. He'd said it was his fault because Arthur had already been caught behind the library once while a woman gave him a handjob. He was lucky he hadn't been caned, but a second infraction that involved sneaking two women up to his room would certainly get him expelled. The Head Dean would never allow that to go unpunished after Arthur had already been in trouble.

Even if they didn't kick him out by some small chance, they might tell Arthur's Mum, and she'd be furious at her son for thinking with the wrong head. She was always nasty to him, and their relationship certainly wouldn't grow any better if he was sent home in shame.

Jasper didn't have parents to hear about anything, and he hadn't been in trouble so far. He had a chance of staying.

The grounds were mostly deserted as Jasper followed Ezra. He only saw two guys by the light of the torches near the fountain toward the front, but they didn't seem to be paying attention. The office building for Professors appeared empty.

Jasper followed Ezra up the stairs to the top floor and into his office. The warm fire illuminated the dark leather furniture, the desk to one side, and the shelves with books. A large looking glass was on the wall by the window.

On the desk, a candle sat in its holder on a stone coaster. Parchment lay scattered about with red ink marks. It was probably essays, and Jasper knew that his was in the pile, but he wasn't so worried about his grade now.

Ezra sat in the leather armchair behind his desk as Jasper stood in front of it. "You know how strict the Head Dean is. No women are allowed into the men's room at any time for any reason. They have the same rule in their building."

"Yes, Sir."

"Are you willing to become a Father at your age?"

"No, Sir."

"It could happen. Even the herbs that some women take aren't foolproof." Ezra leaned back. "This is worse than fooling around in the bushes. You brought two women up there and had someone else involved in your troublemaking."

"I'm sorry, Sir."

"I could cane you and send you back to your room," said Ezra. "I could also tell the Head Dean tomorrow. A lady got in trouble for sneaking a man in through her window last week. And then with Arthur…" he sighed. "He's sick of it, and if trouble keeps happening, he might forbid women again. You'll probably be expelled if I tell the Head Dean."

"It was just one time!" exclaimed Jasper. Nobody could yell at him after he was booted out, but he could almost hear his dead Father slurring at him.

"You'll always be worthless. I built this business from the ground up, and you're willing to piss on it and throw it all away."

Like Jasper wanted the same merchant business that Father had owned. Sure, he'd built it up by hand and amassed quite a fortune, but the stress had also made him an alcoholic. Jasper wasn't inclined to drink like that, but he still hadn't wanted anything to do with it, and when Father's liver had finally given up a few years ago, he'd sold everything. He could live for a while on his savings, and it was paying for College too.

He'd wanted to figure something out for himself, but if he was kicked out, Father would probably laugh from his grave.

Ezra slowly shook his head. "You know that ironclad rule. I'll give you eight strokes and think about whether I should speak to the Head Dean. I could suspend you for a week too and write down a fib for the reasoning if I don't tell him. I think that would be fitting."

Jasper loved Boston College and having something that he could do. Every good mark he got on a test and everything he learned was because *he* put the work in, and nobody could take credit for that.

Missing a week wouldn't be the end of the world, but he'd miss lessons and have to struggle to catch up. Since he didn't have a home elsewhere now, he'd be stuck in his room for the whole week unless he went to the Dining Hall. Everyone would notice he wasn't in class and know he'd done something wrong."

"Wait, I'll do anything," blurted Jasper. "Even if you cane me, please, don't tell the Head Dean or suspend me."

Ezra peered at him. "Anything?"

Jasper nodded, thinking about how much money he had. He could easily pay the Professor a bribe. It wasn't ethical, but money could be quite tempting. He probably wouldn't be able to get out of being caned, and it'd be a struggle to not get aroused while the Professor did something he'd fantasized about, but he'd cross that hurdle when it came.

"I'll do anything," repeated Jasper.

Even if he had to write a hundred essays on why rules should be followed, he'd do it.

Ezra stared at him and was probably imagining that or making Jasper write lines until his hand cramped. Or perhaps he was thinking about how much money he could ask for. Professors shouldn't accept bribes, but it didn't mean it never happened.

"What if we make a deal?" asked Ezra. "You'll accept a special punishment, and I won't suspend you."

"Like what?" asked Jasper.

"For the next few hours, you'll do *whatever* I say with no complaints." Ezra rested his elbows on the armrests as he steepled his fingers. "I have a feeling you truly would do anything I'd ask of you, and that you're that sort."

That sort? Something about his expression said this involved things of a sexual nature. Jasper wouldn't simply be caned and sent back to his room with a sore arse.

"Uh, what would I have to do?" asked Jasper. There was no way…

"Whatever I say," said Ezra. "I won't be cruel, but you'll get more than a caning, that's for sure. In fact, I intend to make your ass quite sore in several ways."

Jasper stared at him. The Professor, who had to be at least thirty-two and ten years older, wanted to fuck him? He'd never thought the Professor was into men.

Bloody hell, was he dreaming? He'd had a few imaginings of Ezra coming onto him in some way, but he always thought they'd remain as fantasies.

"I'd actually rather not tell the Head Dean, and you can say no to a deal, but you'll still be caned, and I'll suspend you," said Ezra. "If you take the deal, no suspension."

Hell, yes, Jasper would do whatever the Professor said. Like he'd say no to having some of his fantasies made true. That was hardly a punishment.

"I'll do it," he said hurriedly.

"Have you ever had pain mixed with your pleasure?"

"Yeah." Jasper's cock twitched, and he dared to say something else. "I like it."

"I had a feeling. Get over here."

Jasper's cock was already stiffening. At least now, he wouldn't have to worry about trying to keep it down while he took the cane.

"Are you going to let me cum?" he asked as he came around the desk.

Ezra stood, grabbed his shoulders, and turned him toward the looking glass on the wall before pulling off his coat. "The main rule besides obeying me is this: While you're serving me, my pleasure comes first, and that should be the main thing on your mind. Yours is secondary." He started plucking at Jasper's vest buttons. "Stay still. If you disobey or I think that you're worried about your own fun and cumming too much, I will halt everything and remind you with whatever implement I choose. This isn't about you simply enjoying yourself. You need to learn a lesson and take your punishment. Punishment is meant to hurt, and it will."

He slid off Jasper's linen shirt and started working his belt. Jasper had expected to be ordered to strip, but being undressed like a doll was somehow even more humiliating.

"If I decide you're not to cum, you won't," added Ezra.

It wasn't a definite no. Jasper's face grew hot as his trousers were slid down, and the Professor's slim fingers grasped his cock for a moment.

"Kick off your shoes."

Once every stitch of clothing was removed from Jasper, Ezra put them all in a desk drawer.

"Bend over the desk."

He pushed Jasper down, not seeming to care about the essays scattered across it. He caught the name on one close by. It was Arthur's, but he forgot about it as his wrists were pulled behind his back. He heard another drawer opening, and a moment later, it felt like thick leather was encasing one wrist. It was buckled on, and once his other wrist was cuffed too, he couldn't pull them apart. There must have been a chain link between them.

"You just keep this stuff in your desk drawer?" Jasper had a feeling he wasn't the first to be bent over like this in here.

"Did I say to speak?"

"Erm, no."

Ezra gave him a good slap on the ass, and he jumped. "No, what?"

"No, Sir."

"Don't slip up again." Ezra pulled something else out from his drawers. A martinet. "Keep quiet."

Jasper didn't get any warning before the leather strips licked across his bare ass. He jumped a little at the sting, but he knew he could handle this. The next came barely two seconds after the first, and the combined sting was worse.

It grew as Ezra timed each lash with two seconds between them so he was feeling the next before the last had dissipated. Jasper couldn't help squirming after the fifteenth.

"Stop moving," ordered Ezra. "Or maybe I should use something else? Shall I do that or are you going to stay still?"

"I'll stay still, Sir."

Ezra struck him again. "Clearly, you already have trouble following the rules."

"This is the first time I got in trouble here!"

Ezra pulled him up to stand and made him lean against the desk as he held the martinet so the strands brushed Jasper's erect cock. Oh shit, he should have kept his mouth shut. It wouldn't leave lasting marks, but certain parts were more delicate than his rear.

"You're here to be disciplined and learn a lesson." Ezra locked eyes with Jasper. "So what are you going to do?"

Jasper swallowed. "Whatever you say, Sir." It took all of his self-control to not attempt to angle his hips away from the martinet or pull to the side.

Ezra took him by the throat, and the simple gesture and feel of a hand on the delicate skin made pre-cum bead on the tip of his cock. He glanced down and saw the Professor was aroused too.

"Look me in the eye," said Ezra. Jasper did and flinched as the leather struck him. He wasn't sure what to make of the sensation in so many sensitive places at once. A few of the strands had struck his cock and balls, and several had gone across his pelvic area and lower abdomen.

His breathing picked up a little. It was still bearable, but he wished he'd kept his mouth so he'd get the leather on his ass instead.

"You'll definitely pay attention now, won't you?" asked Ezra.

"Yes, Sir."

"Pain is great for teaching naughty students a lesson, but they must focus on it and allow it in," said Ezra. "They must agree that they deserve punishment for the infraction regardless of how well-behaved they were *before*. You're being disciplined because you did something *now*."

Ezra flicked his wrists again, and the tails of the martinet landed on all of Jasper's most sensitive spots.

"Did you break a rule?"

"Yes, Sir." The leather hit again.

"Do you deserve to be punished for what you did wrong?"

"Yes, Sir." The strands struck.

"Are you going to sneak women into your room again?"

"No, Sir." Another strike. Jasper tried to keep his hips still.

"Do you wholeheartedly believe you deserve this punishment?"

Jasper actually hadn't done anything wrong unless touching a woman's breasts counted. But he certainly wasn't tattling on Arthur, and the Professor's eyes, which hadn't left his the whole time, wasn't something he wanted to end. The gaze and being at the Professor's mercy made his stomach flutter with excitement

"I deserve it, Sir. Please punish me, Sir."

"Then take it," whispered Ezra.

Jasper held perfectly still as Ezra continued with the martinet. He didn't count the strokes or wonder how many were left. He just took it while Ezra's hand remained around his throat and the greyish-blue eyes stayed on his.

He'd probably taken a dozen when Ezra finally stopped and dropped the martinet on the desk. Jasper trembled a bit as the Professor's cool hands rubbed his balls and hips to take away the lingering sting before he leaned in and kissed Jasper.

He hadn't been expecting that, but he kissed back. Another fantasy made true. It was hard, demanding, and something he'd expect from an older man with more experience. He also detected a hint of mint and lemon. They weren't two scents he'd choose to mix, but on the Professor, it seemed so right.

Ezra pulled back too soon as he grasped Jasper's raging erection and ran his thumb over the damp slit. "Get under the desk and on your knees. Someone's coming in a bit, and you'll remain quiet while you suck my cock."

Jasper's eyes widened, and he opened his mouth to say something, but Ezra put a finger to his lips.

"Not a word of complaint."

His eyes said the martinet on his cock and balls was nothing compared to what else he might do if Jasper balked. The potential sparked excitement, but he wanted to obey.

Once he was in place, Ezra sat and scooted his chair closer to the desk.

"You can't suck me off if my dick's tucked in my trousers. Get to work."

Jasper heard parchment slide across the desk as he bent his head. The meaning was pretty clear, and his hands were useless, so there was only one way to do this. This was for Ezra's pleasure, not that Jasper wouldn't enjoy it, but even for this, he'd have to work for it.

He used his teeth to tug on the laces. Once they were loosened enough, he pulled on the trouser fabric to move it and gently took the top of the Professor's drawers in his mouth to pull them down. It took more work, but finally, Ezra's erection was free.

He was definitely going to need plenty of oil in his ass to take that. The foreskin had pulled back a little to reveal the head that glistened wetly.

Jasper let out a small sigh as he flicked his tongue out to taste it. How many times had he fantasized about sucking off his English Professor? Now, he could actually do it. He took the head in his mouth, and the Professor spoke.

"My cock better not leave your mouth for any reason whatsoever."

Jasper made a noise to show he understood as he savored the taste.

"And if you don't do a good job, perhaps you'll find out what the cane feels like on your balls."

Jasper had one purpose right now, and he'd happily fulfill it. He took the length in his throat with ease since his bed buddy had trained him well.

Even though he wasn't being directly stimulated by it, he loved sucking cock. A couple of his early, quick encounters a few years ago had taught him that. Thankfully, the Professor kept that area neat so Jasper didn't have to worry about hairs getting in his mouth.

The Professor's quill scratched away as he presumably made notes on an essay. How could he focus while Jasper bobbed his head like his life depended on making Ezra cum?

"I swear, some of these students come up with the most outlandish things," Ezra muttered so low, Jasper almost didn't hear him. "And that's not how you spell hypothesis."

Thank God that wasn't Jasper's essay. After a minute, Ezra reached under the desk to stroke Jasper's head. He couldn't help the noise of pleasure he let out as the Professor lightly scratched his scalp.

"Keep quiet," murmured Ezra.

The door opened a moment later, and the Professor removed his hand. Jasper almost paused since normally, someone walking in while he had a cock in his mouth would be bad news. But he was completely hidden, so he kept sucking as Ezra and the stranger greeted each other.

"I just got back, but here it is. Look at how thick it is."

Ezra's shaft was definitely thick, but Jasper took it down his throat.

"It'll take me a while to read through that." Ezra's voice was completely normal as if his cock wasn't completely sheathed in the warm mouth of one of his students. "How much do I owe you?"

Jasper flicked his tongue on the underside while Ezra opened a drawer. Coins clinked, and the man spoke about other works a bookseller had.

"It was a long trip, but worth it," he finished. "He says he'll get more stuff soon, so if you have anything else in mind, let me know. I'll probably go back next month and see what else I can add to my collection."

Jasper's neglected cock leaked pre-cum as he kept at his task. Their secret gave him tingles in his stomach. What if the man knew and wanted to watch? The idea was so thrilling, he almost wished it would happen. It was a fantasy he'd thought of before, and this was the closest he'd ever gotten.

Ezra's hand pushed his head down, forcing him to take it all in and hold it. "I've got more essays to finish grading, and it's late, but I thank you for the trouble."

"It's no trouble at all. Like I'd ever complain about book hunting." The man chuckled. "I'll see you later."

Jasper listened as footsteps headed for the door. Air would be nice now. The door closed, and he had a feeling Ezra was testing him, so he remained still and compliant since he wasn't desperate.

The Professor finally pulled him back enough to breathe. "Good boy."

They both continued at their task, although Ezra had to be close since he seemed to grow a little tense.

"Fuck."

He probably wasn't paying much attention to the essays now. He leaned back, and Jasper looked up from under his lashes. His jaw was a little sore, and his eyes were watery, but he didn't slow down.

Ezra fisted his hair as his breathing grew ragged. "Fuck, I'm about to-"

He didn't finish. Jasper tasted cum as thick ropes of it spurted into his mouth. He couldn't help the groan of excitement as he tasted the salty fluid and felt the Professor tensing under him.

Ezra bucked his hips as a last bit came out. As he breathed and finally relaxed, he stroked Jasper's hair while he swallowed the cum and lapped at the head to get every last bit.

Without another word, Ezra sat up and continued working. Jasper had been told to keep the cock in his mouth no matter what, and he hadn't been told to do anything else, so he simply stayed in place.

The Professor's dick softened as he graded. Jasper thought he'd be told to lift his head or something by now, but five minutes turned into ten. He shifted a little as his knees grew sore.

"Stay still," Ezra said with a warning note. "Think about what you did to deserve your punishment and what you should be focusing on."

He must have liked the feel of a warm mouth around his soft cock besides degrading his student. Jasper was being punished, so his wants didn't matter. It was kind of hard to think of his "transgression" since he hadn't bribed the guard. That had been Arthur. Perhaps he should have told, but that was tattling and quite low. Some friend he'd be.

Still, this was a lesson on obedience and doing as he was told, something he always craved in bed. He shouldn't be wishing for something to alleviate his boredom or fidgeting. He was supposed to focus on Ezra's pleasure.

Fifteen minutes passed, and Ezra finally pushed his chair back. Jasper had to follow on his knees since he was pretty sure letting go with his mouth would earn him punishment.

Ezra's lips twitched in a faint smile before he stood and stepped to the side. Jasper had to walk on his knees to stay with him. Slowly, so his student could keep up, he started walking backward.

Jasper followed on his knees, not daring to let the Professor's cock slip from his mouth. It twitched slightly, and he had a feeling Ezra quite enjoyed leading him along like a pet on a leash.

Ezra took him all the way to the leather armchairs by the fire. "Let go. What do you say?"

Jasper finally got to fully close his mouth for a moment. "Thank you for letting me suck your cock, Sir."

"And?"

"Er, thank you for teaching me to keep still and focus on you, Sir."

Ezra grabbed a throw blanket from one of the armchairs and draped it over the ottoman. "Bend over that. While I cane you, keep quiet, and don't move or I'll really give you something to howl and squirm about."

And he'd probably be sent to his room later with full, achy balls. He'd have to jerk himself off once Arthur was asleep.

He settled his upper body across the ottoman. Rustles came from behind him, and he finally heard footsteps. Ezra got down behind him and pressed himself against Jasper as if they were about to fuck.

He was completely naked and erect. Jasper's cock had calmed earlier, but it started to thicken again as he automatically ground his ass against Ezra. The Professor's lips touched the back of his neck.

"Soon," he whispered.

He stood, and Jasper felt the cane brush his ass. This would hurt worse than the martinet, and he'd have marks.

They'd probably last for a good week, and he'd feel them every time he sat or shifted in his seat. This night would be stuck in his memory for a long time, and he'd probably wank to it several times. A few seconds passed as he waited and tried not to tense. His fuck buddy had said he shouldn't clench his arse to try and save himself the pain, and he had a feeling Ezra wouldn't like that either.

The cane struck without warning. Jasper barely kept a gasp in as the sudden pain bit into his bare bottom. It seemed to radiate through his rear. Five seconds passed before the next hit a little lower. He stared at the fire as the third hit. He was tempted to clench just before the next one, but he kept himself relaxed.

He wasn't supposed to count or think about how many he had left. He took the next hit, and the one after seemed to come a little quicker.

It struck where his ass met his thighs, and he was tempted to swear. He pressed his lips together as he felt a tingle of nerves from the pleasant anticipation. The next was coming.

The cane hit the back of his thighs which were more sensitive, and he couldn't help but make a slight noise. His cock was like a post, and he was sure if Ezra had simply punished him earlier instead of making their deal, he never would have been able to keep himself down.

Another weal was made on his thighs, and he was struggling to not tense up then. While the pain radiated, nothing happened. So many seconds passed, he wondered if Ezra was satisfied, and that was it.

A diagonal strike came across his arse, and it crossed the earlier ones. That one made him suck in a breath as he broke out in a light sweat.

"It's done," said Ezra, and he knelt by Jasper to sweep his fingers across the weals. "You took that quite well."

Jasper couldn't help the faint sense of pride, although it wasn't so much directed at himself. He'd pleased Ezra and done as he was told. The Professor stood and moved away, presumably to tuck the cane in his desk and fetch oil. He took so long, Jasper's erection flagged a bit, although he knew what was coming.

He knew from experience that being fucked after a beating on his bottom could hurt the fresh marks, although it was something he enjoyed, and the pain wasn't as sharp across the skin either.

Ezra returned and got behind him so his cock brushed Jasper's ass. "Do you know what intercrural is?"

"Yes, Sir," said Jasper.

"I haven't decided if I'll let you cum yet, and I have a feeling you'll be a bit too fast. Unless you're good at holding back. Are you?"

"Only to a point, Sir," replied Jasper. "After a bit…I just can't, Sir."

Ezra rubbed his shoulders, and Jasper felt his breath puffing on the back of his neck. "At least you're honest."

Partly. This whole experience was because of a lie, but he couldn't even feel guilty with the feel of the Professor's body against him.

Ezra's oiled finger carefully slipped into his ass. Jasper couldn't help but to wiggle slightly. He'd thought about the Professor's hands on him in so many ways and never thought any of those fantasies would come true.

The Professor made sure Jasper's thighs were close together after he rubbed some oil on the inner part. Jasper had only done this once when he was too nervous to get fucked up the ass with some random guy he met at the tavern since he'd still been a virgin. It only brought pleasure if the giver reached around to jerk the receiver.

As the Professor's cock slipped between his thighs, he knew he wouldn't be getting jerked, or at least not yet.

The Professor didn't start thrusting. Instead, he slipped a second oiled finger into Jasper's hole to stretch him further. As he worked his student's hole, his fingers kept brushing the sweet spot, and Jasper had to make an effort to not move.

"It'd be fun to leave you wanting," said Ezra. "In fact, I think I will."

Jasper squeezed his eyes shut and tried not to curse in his head. This was for Ezra's pleasure, not his. He'd have to accept whatever was done without complaints even though the stimulation in his ass might drive him up a wall if he wasn't allowed to finish. A third finger was added.

"You've been good, but not allowing you to cum will hammer the lesson in." Ezra added more oil and buried his fingers in Jasper's ass once more. "I intend to finish in you and send you back to your room with my cum in your ass."

Jasper made a slight noise that he couldn't help as his cock throbbed. To be sent out and have to walk back while feeling the Professor's cum leak out of him…maybe he should misbehave again.

"I bet if I told you to not touch yourself for a week, you'd do it even though I'd have no real way to know." Ezra leaned down as his fingers plunged in and out, and he directly massaged the sweet spot as he licked the outer edge of Jasper's ear. "Wouldn't you?"

The combined stimulation made him jerk, and he knew the answer. "Y-yes, Sir."

"Why? You could do it in secret. It's not like I can be hovering over you all day."

"Because-" Jasper squirmed as the pressure back there grew heavier, and the Professor's free hand reached around to grasp his cock although he didn't jerk it. "I'd do it to please you. I'd rather be honest about it."

"Good boy. You like doing as you're told, don't you?"

"Yes, Sir."

Jasper tensed as he struggled to not thrust into the hand gripping him. It went away too soon, and the Professor slipped his fingers out before he started thrusting. Jasper kept his thighs together as tight as he could to make it snug for him. It certainly wasn't the same as an ass, but judging by the way the Professor gripped his student's hips, he was enjoying himself.

Jasper tried to put his thighs closer although he was pretty sure he couldn't. Still, anything to make it better for the Professor. Ezra had been erect earlier when Jasper was being punished at the desk, and waiting must have been hard for him too. He probably wouldn't last that long.

The thrusting was making Jasper's cock rub against the blanket over the ottoman, although it wasn't enough to get him off. It was more like a tease if anything. Ezra suddenly pulled back after a couple of minutes, and Jasper felt cool oil drip down his crack.

"I need to be in your ass." Ezra started working the head in. "Is this what you imagined before? Hmm?"

"What, Sir?" Jasper managed to get out as he bore down and pushed back a little. His heart rate picked up a bit.

Ezra slowly slid himself in. "You think I didn't notice a couple of times when you must have let your mind wander in class, and I caught you staring at me?"

Jasper's face flamed as he pushed back more, desperate for every inch. "Uh, no, Sir."

Ezra let out a strained snort as he leaned down and started with slow thrusts. "I noticed. Is this what you were imagining? Tell me what you thought."

"I thought...fuck-" Jasper's cock throbbed as pre-cum dribbled out. "I thought about you bending me over your desk...and fucking my brains out, Sir. Or my desk, or anywhere, Sir. And caning me."

Ezra reached around to grasp Jasper's cock. His thumb rubbed the slick head. "Is that what you imagine when you touch yourself?"

"Yes, Sir. Oh, God, please fuck me harder, Sir."

The Professor's pace increased. For several moments, Jasper's whole world consisted of Ezra's cock in his ass, Ezra's hand on his cock, and Ezra's breath and grunts against his neck. It was all Ezra, and he didn't ever want it to end. The pressure built as the Professor pounded his ass and smeared the pre-cum around his head.

"Sir-I'm going to cum," Jasper forced out even though he didn't want anything to stop.

Ezra wrapped his arms around Jasper's torso to pull him closer and snaked a hand up to lightly grasp his throat. "Then cum for me, my sweet boy."

"What?" Jasper wasn't allowed. He must have misheard.

"Cum on my cock, Jasper. I need to feel it."

He was so close, he was sure he couldn't have pulled back even if he wanted to now. The Professor's slow, clear words, and the slick feel of his tongue against the rim of Jasper's ear sent him over the edge.

"Oh, God, Ezra!" he shouted as he involuntarily clenched.

The Professor sucked in a breath as his thrusts grew faster and erratic. The orgasm seemed to explode from inside of Jasper as the special spot was repeatedly stroked.

"That's it...cum on my cock like a good boy," gasped Ezra.

The order and being called a good boy somehow made it more intense. Jasper's hips jerked as he came all over the blanket. Ezra thrusted himself to the hilt and groaned as he filled his student's hole with cum. Even though he was in as far as he could go, he still pushed like it would never be enough.

Jasper pushed back against him, also somehow wanting more. He wanted to hold onto the moment forever and stay in it, but the orgasm started to fade. A last dribble cum hit the blanket

"Fuck," Ezra swore as he gave a final twitch.

Jasper had gone limp on the ottoman, and he felt the Professor's head rest on his shoulder. His cock was still buried in Jasper's hole, but it slowly started to soften. He shifted himself to pull out and stayed against his student.

The afterglow was always nice, but Jasper figured he'd be hurried out in a few seconds. Ezra stayed on him longer than he expected, but he finally got up.

"Stay there."

Rustles came from the desk, and Jasper soon felt something slightly cold on his bottom.

"It's balm," said Ezra. "That's all. You'll definitely be feeling these weals for a week, but this will help tonight."

After he smoothed it on, he undid the cuffs, and Jasper started to sit up, but Ezra's hand on his lower back kept him down. Some of the cum had dribbled out of his ass, but the Professor wiped him with a cloth.

It was a little humiliating to be cleaned but somehow soothing. Jasper's fuck buddy upstairs had never done anything like this. As soon as they were done, Jasper was expected to deal with himself. Hell, the other guy never even thought to put anything on the marks left behind. Jasper had a little jar of balm in his bedside drawer that he could put on in private, so someone else caring for him was a new experience.

But certainly not unwelcome. In fact, he wanted this again. Punishment. Sex. Being used like a toy but still taken care of afterward. He'd never had such a night with anyone, and he didn't want this to be his last.

"Did you learn your lesson?" asked Ezra.

"Yes, Sir." Jasper hastily spoke before he lost his nerve. "But...maybe you should do this again to make sure."

Ezra pulled away the cloth and rubbed his ass, moist from the balm. "This wasn't enough?"

"I was thinking maybe I should have weekly reminders to make sure I don't forget."

Ezra gently took his arm to make him straighten up before embracing and kissing him.

As his tongue invaded Jasper's mouth in a rough kiss, he wasn't sure if that was a yes or no. In case it was a no, he let himself be lost in it as his tongue clashed with the Professor's. Ezra lightly sucked on his bottom lip before he drew his head back.

"I can definitely give you reminders," he said with a smile.

Jasper returned it as he gently scratched the Professor's back. "I'll need plenty of reminders."

"That sounds good. Now, come here. You're not going back to your room quite just yet."

He wasn't?

Ezra wrapped him in another throw blanket and sat in one of the armchairs while he held Jasper.

"What are you doing?"

Ezra raised an eyebrow. "Did you think I'd have you get dressed and plunk you in the hall as soon as we were done?"

"Er, yes," replied Jasper. No one else had cuddled with him like this afterward except for ladies, but he'd only had plain sex with them.

Ezra shook his head. "You haven't had many good lovers have you?"

"Well...they weren't terrible in bed."

"It's not just the sex. It's what happens afterward. You don't whip or cane someone and send them off without a backward glance. They might be fine later, but they might not. All of the heightened sensations from pain and pleasure mixed can be too much. Your mind is flying high for a bit-" Ezra raised his hand. "After the orgasm and everything stops, it can drop for some." He lowered his hand. "I would never play with someone and then quickly boot them out."

"Oh. I didn't know that. I never felt horrible afterward."

"Not everybody gets it, but some do. It's not always right away either, so if you feel off or down later, come see me, okay? Even if it's three in the morning, do it. I don't want you to feel like that and be alone. It's not healthy for the mind, and whoever does the whipping and tying has a responsibility to make sure the receiver is fine afterward."

"I will." Jasper had never heard of such a thing. Maybe having an older lover would be better because he obviously knew more and was experienced at such things. Ezra would be careful with more than his body. "And this is nice. I like it."

Ezra rubbed his arm. "If we'll be doing this again, I want to make something clear. You don't get special privileges in class, all right? You still have to do the same work as everyone else, and I'll grade you just like the rest."

"I know," said Jasper. "I don't want good marks just handed over to me. I like working for them. Can I still have help outside of class time if I need it? I'm having trouble with poetry."

"I'll always help my students. Bring your work to me tomorrow after lunch. I have some books you can borrow too. But since you learned your lesson, make sure you remind Arthur of the rules. It's not to hound you, but if there's too much trouble between both sides, the women might get kicked out again. I don't want that."

"I'll remind him," said Jasper. "I don't want them to be kicked out either."

"And for the future, I don't like denying orgasms too much. You seem to like pleasing, and I reward good boys."

Jasper smiled as he ran his hand across the Professor's bare chest. "I am a pleaser in bed. I thought I'd have to bribe you with money. I wasn't expecting this."

"You're a good student, and you shouldn't be kicked out for a first offense. If you hadn't wanted the deal, I would have simply given you a few strokes of the cane as punishment and sent you back to your room with a suspension. You would behave in the future, wouldn't you?"

"I would." Jasper covered his face. "If you weren't into men…the caning still would have made me hard. Dear God. That would be humiliating if you were straight."

Ezra snorted. "You wouldn't be the first. Even straight men have had that…surprise. The polite thing would be to pretend it hadn't happened."

Jasper suddenly thought of something. "Wait, how did you know we were in there?"

"One of Jane's friends came to tattle to me, so I went up, and sure enough, there you all were."

Jasper's mouth dropped. "Jane's friend?"

"I guess she told her and thought she'd keep quiet about it. Don't ask which one."

"Well, I can't say I'm mad at her if it led to this."

***

When Jasper returned to his room, Arthur was still awake.

"You're not getting expelled, are you?" he asked as he hastily stood from his bed.

"No. I'm not."

"You were gone for quite a bit."

Jasper couldn't tell his friend the truth or that he'd be getting fucked by their English Professor every week for the foreseeable future. "I got the lecture of the century on morals and rules, and he threatened to cane me if I step a toe out of line again. I'm supposed to remind you of them too because if there's too much trouble with the men and women fooling around, all of the women might get kicked out."

Arthur sat on the edge of the bed. "I didn't really think of that."

Jasper pulled back the curtain so he could still see Arthur as he sat on his bed. "I know you really like Jane...but beyond not doing this again to stay out of trouble, maybe you should be careful with her. She told some buddy of hers that she'd be sneaking over here with the other girl, and the supposed buddy told Ezra."

Arthur pressed his lips together for a moment as his eyes widened. "She went and snitched?!"

"Yeah." Jasper rolled his eyes.

"Which one?"

"He wouldn't tell me. If someone goes to him, he can't really be saying who. That could cause a lot of trouble. It must be one of the goody-goodies hoping to gain favor."

Arthur huffed and fiddled with his earring. "I'll tell her she needs to be careful about what she tells her friends. I won't sneak her or anyone up again. I'm sorry you got your ear chewed off. I owe you big time."

Jasper chuckled as he stood to draw the curtain again so he could undress. "You can buy me a drink the next time we go out."

"I'll buy you drinks for a month. He probably would have expelled me for that since I already got in trouble once."

Jasper lay on his stomach once the lanterns were out, and he was in bed. He'd only wanted to keep Arthur out of trouble and at the college so he didn't have to go home to his bitchy Mum. He didn't expect a lesson on submitting and care.

What else would he learn in the future?

Lessons II

Arthur's Lesson

After a session with Will that leads to a physical altercation, Arthur knows his time at Boston College may be near its end. Will plans to tell things to the Head Dean if Arthur won't agree to his demands. Perhaps Jasper and Ezra can help him.

Jasper and Arthur's Lessons

When Ezra learns that Jasper has the same fantasy as him, he suggests that Arthur could help. A third in the mix might lead to new lessons and a HEA for all.

Buy   now

Other works by Julie Mannino

For info on the latest books, including queer fairy tales, fantasy, and M/M romance, sign up here for the Newsletter.

Jack's Day (Jack's Reign Book One)

Chloe's Purpose (Jack's Reign Book Two)

Eado's Birth (Jack's Reign Book Three)

Leon the Lion (Jack's Reign Side Novel)

A Royal Obsession

The Grey Wolf

M/M Tippy the Knight An Erotic Short Story

LGBTQIA+ Loki's Price
M/M Angel Devil A Thrall Short Story
M/M Thrall A Novel of Alternate Earth

LGBTQIA+ Finley's Way
M/M The Hunted

M/M Secrets
M/M Secrets II

M/M Promises

M/M Valentine (An Asexual M/M Fairy Romance)

M/M Lessons (An MM Dark Academia College Romance)
M/M Lessons II (An MM Dark Academia College Romance)

Alternate Earth Tales-M/M Fairytales

Little Red Riding Hood
Cynric Ella

Printed in Great Britain
by Amazon